A NOTE FROM THE AUTHOR

When I was small, the kitchen was the place I felt the most coddled, cosy and happy. Baking with Mum was one of my favourite things. I had her all to myself and we would chat about school and sing silly songs.

I would lick the bowl and she would wipe my face. Teamwork.

Jess Mikhail draws the pictures

Eva Katzler writes the stories

I grew up with two busy working parents, but they always had time for me. Whether I was cleaning the candlesticks with Mum (polishing pirates' treasure) or helping Dad tidy up the garden (chatting to pixies in the forest), I was playing, enjoying being with my parents and having the time of my life.

Florentine and Pig is a safe, imaginative and fun-filled world, which encourages families to read, play and create together. It celebrates the imagination of little ones and champions parents' loving and creative relationships with their children.

I cherish my childhood memories and I hope that Florentine and Pig will inspire parents to fill their own children's memory banks with silly times, messy times and most importantly, good fun family times.

I can't wait to hear all about them . . .

All the recipes and crafts in this book have been designed for children to make with help from a responsible adult, so grab your aprons and sticky tape and jump on board!

Eva X

Laura and Jess Tilli make up the recipes and arty bits

For more recipes, crafts and ideas, please pop over to **www.florentineandpig.com** or become our fan on Facebook

Remember, sharp knives and hot things can be dangerous.
Adults should supervise children closely when cooking and crafting.

To Mum, Dad and Benchick.
Bestest team everest – E.K.

To Kathleen, who also likes to
dance whilst cooking – J.M.

Bloomsbury Publishing,
London, Berlin, New York and Sydney

First published in Great Britain in June 2012 by Bloomsbury Publishing Plc
50 Bedford Square, London, WC1B 3DP

Text copyright © Florentine and Pig Ltd 2012
Illustrations copyright © Jess Mikhail 2012
Recipes devised and crafts co-devised by Laura and Jess Tilli
Wallpaper design reproduced by kind permission of Elanbach
The moral rights of the author and illustrator have been asserted

A CIP catalogue record for this book is available from the British Library

ISBN 978 1 4088 2939 4 (HB)
ISBN 978 1 4088 2437 5 (PB)

FSC
www.fsc.org
MIX
Paper from
responsible sources
FSC® C008047

C&C Offset Printing Co Ltd, Shenzhen, Guangdong

1 3 5 7 9 10 8 6 4 2

All papers used by Bloomsbury Publishing are natural,
recyclable products made from wood grown in well-managed forests.
The manufacturing processes conform to the environmental
regulations of the country of origin

www.bloomsbury.com
www.florentineandpig.com

Florentine and Pig Have a Very Lovely Picnic

Eva Katzler

Illustrated by Jess Mikhail

Recipes and crafts by Laura and Jess Tilli

BLOOMSBURY

LONDON BERLIN NEW YORK SYDNEY

Florentine and Pig were having breakfast one sparkly morning. 'Now that the sun is warm and toasty, I think we should do something lovely outdoors,' said Florentine.

'Oh, Pig, I have a wonderful idea! We should have a picnic!'

Pig liked the sound of a picnic very much indeed.

'We need to think of our favourite things to eat,' Florentine said.
'I love runny honey and YOU love crunchy apples.'

Florentine began scribbling
in her notebook.

The pencil was moving so
speedy fast it made Pig's
eyes go big and funny.

Florentine and Pig's
very lovely picnic

Apple + carrot muffins with
sunshine lemon icing

Rainbow sprinkle cookies

Cheddar cheese + pumpkin seed bites

Sticky red onion hummus with cucumber dunkers

Green pea picnic-time tarts

Florentine's home-made pink lemonade
with fresh berry ice cubes

At last, Florentine revealed all the
marvellous things they would make.

Pig's eyes got bigger and blinkier.

He thought Florentine was really rather
clever to think up such a lovely picnic.

'Oh no, Pig!'
Florentine gasped.
'You ate our very last
apple for breakfast!'

'How will we ever make our muffins now?'

Just as Florentine had said, Pig could
not see any more apples on their
apple tree.

'Oh dear,' said Florentine.
'What are we going to do? Pig?'

'Pig?'

'Pig, where
are you?'

Florentine couldn't
see Pig anywhere!

Just then, Pig burst back into the kitchen with such a crash that all the pots and pans wobbled and rang and clattered and banged!

He was carrying his shiny telescope!

He pointed it at their apple tree, shut one eye
and peered through the telescope with the other.

(Pig was really rather good at winking.)

Suddenly, Pig began jumping in the air excitedly!
'What is it, Pig?' Florentine asked. 'What can you see?'

Right at the very tippy-top of their apple tree were three of the **biggest, reddest, juiciest** and **crunchiest** apples she had ever seen.

'Well I never!' exclaimed Florentine.

'Those apples look very tricky to reach, Pig,' said Florentine. 'How ever will we get them down?'

But Pig was already marching around the kitchen collecting everything he needed for his crunchy apple mission.

Pig loved apples very much indeed, and nothing – but nothing – was going to stop him from having them for his lovely picnic.

Nothing at all.

Florentine and Pig set off into the garden with everything they needed (and a strawberry jam sandwich too, in case Pig got hungry along the way).

Armed with his wooden spoon, Pig waved goodbye to Florentine and disappeared up the ladder.

'You're ever so brave, Pig,' called Florentine from under the tree. 'Do be careful, won't you?'

Florentine watched and listened . . .

She heard **rustling** and **bustling** as Pig bravely bashed the big leaves out of his way with his wooden spoon.

She heard **bumping** and **thumping** as the tree branches **banged** against the bowl on Pig's head.

She heard **chomping** and **chewing** as Pig munched on his strawberry jam sandwich.

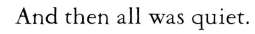

And then all was quiet.

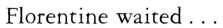

Florentine waited . . .

and waited . . .

and waited.

But she couldn't hear **anything at all.**

'ARE YOU OK, PIG?'
Florentine shouted up.
'ARE YOU STUCK?'

After a moment there was a loud
rustling and a wild swishing of
the leaves at the top of the tree.
Florentine suddenly heard
three very loud snaps.

SNAP!

SNAP!

SNAP!

Then . . . there was

a great thrashing

and a thwacking

and a crashing

and a whooshing!

When Florentine looked up, she glimpsed a flash of red and white spottiness tumbling through the tree towards the ground!

'Oh dear,' said Florentine.

When all the noise had stopped, Florentine peeked through her fingers.

She could see the rope swinging gently at the bottom of the tree, and hanging at the end of it was a very happy . . .

upside-down Pig.

Bundled up inside Pig's tablecloth were three very red . . . very juicy . . . very crunchy . . . apples!

'Oh, Pig, you are clever,'
said Florentine. 'Now we have
everything we need! Let's go
inside and start cooking.'

They rolled up their sleeves, they washed their hands . . .
and then they were ready to begin!

Florentine **baked**
and **caked**
and **mixed**
and **whipped**,

Pig **slurped**
and **sloshed**
and **laughed**
and **licked**!

Florentine **chopped**
and **chunked**
and **danced**
and **diced**,

Pig **whisked**
and **wiggled**
and **stirred**
and **sliced!**

Florentine **dipped**
and **dunked**
and **cooked**
and **crunched,**

and they **tossed**
and **twirled**
and **mashed**
and **munched!**

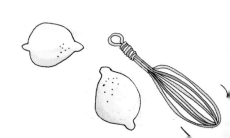

When everything was ready, they laid their blanket beneath the apple tree and brought out all the delicious food they had made.

Florentine and Pig were very happy indeed.

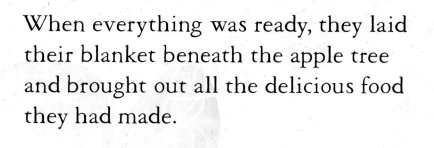

Florentine sighed happily. 'What a very lovely picnic we have had, Pig,' she said. 'I have loved every single minute!'

But Pig was already fast asleep and snoring rather loudly.

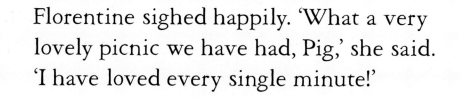

Florentine giggled.

It was then that she noticed
Pig had something . . .

. . . right on the end of his nose.

The End . . . Ta da

Apple and Carrot Muffins with Sunshine Lemon Icing

Makes 6

For the muffins

75g brown sugar
75g soft butter
1 free range egg
1 tbsp natural yoghurt
125g self-raising flour
1 tsp baking powder
1 apple (cored and grated)
1 carrot (peeled and grated)
1 tsp cinnamon

For the icing

75g cream cheese
300g icing sugar
Juice of half a lemon

1 Preheat your oven to 180°C/350°F/gas mark 4.

2 Beat the sugar and butter together in a big bowl with a wooden spoon until it's nice and creamy.

3 Add the egg and yoghurt and mix again.

4 Mix in the flour, baking powder, apple, carrot and cinnamon.

5 Line a muffin tin with 6 muffin cases and plop a big dessertspoonful of your mixture into each case.

6 Pop in the oven for 25 minutes or until lightly golden. (When you poke a skewer into the middle of a muffin and it comes out clean you know they're done!)

7 Whilst you leave them to cool on a wire rack, mix all your icing ingredients together until smooth and creamy.

8 Dollop the icing on top of your delicious muffins and enjoy! Yum!

The muffins may sink a bit when they come out of the oven, but don't worry!

Rainbow Sprinkle Cookies

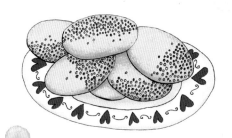

Makes 12

For the cookies
220g soft butter
110g caster sugar
275g plain flour

For the rainbows
3 tbsp icing sugar
Juice of half a lemon
1 tub of hundreds and thousands
or sugar strands

1. Preheat your oven to 180°C/350°F/gas mark 4.

2. Put the butter and sugar into a big bowl and beat with a wooden spoon until soft and creamy.

3. Add the flour, mixing with a spoon first, then when it gets doughy get your hands in the bowl and bring it together into a big doughy ball.

4. Divide the mixture into twelve pieces the size of ping-pong balls and place on a baking sheet, flattening them a bit with your hands.

5. Pop in the oven for 15 minutes or until lightly golden, then cool on a wire rack.

6. To make your rainbows, mix the icing sugar and lemon juice until smooth and tip your sprinkles into a separate bowl.

7. Dip half of each cooled cookie into the icing and then into the sprinkles, then place them on a tray to set. Delicious!

Cheddar Cheese and Pumpkin Seed Bites

Makes 6

You will need

100g rolled oats
100g grated cheddar cheese
50g soft butter
1 small handful of pumpkin seeds
2 tsp chopped fresh rosemary
(or 1 tsp dried)
1 free range egg, beaten

1 Preheat your oven to
180°C/350°F/gas mark 4.

2 In a big bowl, mix all the
ingredients together really well
until you've got a big cheesy,
seedy mixture.

3 Line a muffin tray with 6
cases and divide the mixture
between them.

4 Pop in the oven for
30 minutes or until golden brown.

5 Leave to cool (don't worry if
the egg has made little bubbles on
them – they will soon disappear!)
then gobble them all up with your
best friends.

Pig's Pretty Picnic Bunting

You will need
A triangle of cardboard as a template
Scraps of pretty paper and card –
wallpaper, wrapping paper, napkins,
doilies, whatever you can find!
Scissors
String
Glue

1 Use your template to draw triangles on all your scraps of paper.

2 Carefully cut out all the triangles.

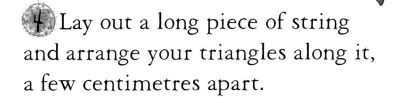

3 If the paper is plain on one side you can stick two triangles together back-to-back with glue.

4 Lay out a long piece of string and arrange your triangles along it, a few centimetres apart.

5 Make sure the string is on top of the straight edge of each triangle, not across the point.

6 Fold the edge of each triangle over to hide the string and stick it down with glue.

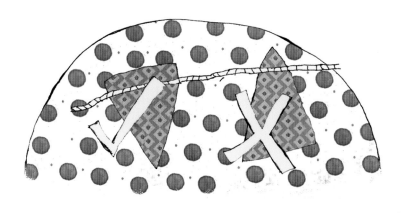

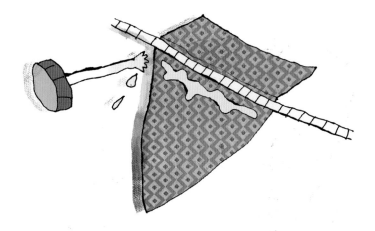

You're done! Now hang your pretty bunting up in the garden or wherever you're having your lovely picnic!

Sticky Red Onion Hummus with Cucumber Dunkers

For the sticky onions
1 red onion
2 tsp sugar
100ml balsamic vinegar
50ml water

For the hummus
1 x 240g tin of chickpeas, drained
4 tbsp olive oil
Juice of half a lemon
Pinch of salt and pepper
1 clove of garlic, peeled and
squashed with the back of a spoon

For the dunkers
Half a cucumber, cut into dunkers

1. Carefully slice your onion as thin as you can and put it in a non-stick pan with the sugar, vinegar and water.

2. Bubble on a very low heat for 20 minutes or until you have a sticky goo. Be very careful not to touch the mixture at this stage as it gets piping hot! Turn the heat off and leave to cool.

3. Put all the ingredients for the hummus into a big bowl and whizz with a hand blender. (Or mash well with a potato masher.)

4. Spoon your hummus into a bowl and pile your sticky onions on top.

5. Arrange your cucumber dunkers on a plate and dunk away!

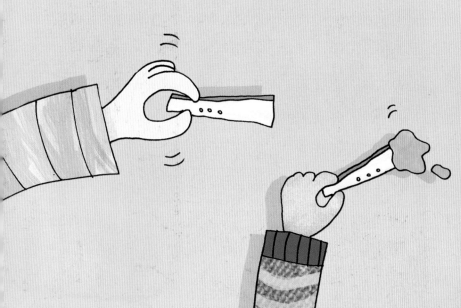

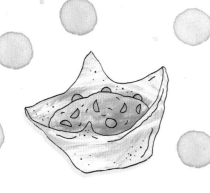

Green pea picnic-time Tarts

Makes 6

For the tarts

6 slices of granary bread,
crusts cut off (just this once!)
Olive oil spray
1 free range egg, beaten
60ml crème fraiche
A big handful of freshly grated
parmesan cheese
60g frozen peas, defrosted
1 spring onion, snipped into small
pieces with scissors (make sure
you use the green bits too!)

1 Preheat your oven to
180°C/350°F/gas mark 4.

2 Using your hands, flatten each
piece of bread slightly and spray
both sides with the olive oil.

3 Line each hollow of a muffin
tray with one slice of bread and
pop in the oven for 10 minutes
until the bread is just starting
to turn golden.

4 In a jug, mix together the
egg, crème fraiche and most of
the grated cheese.

5 Divide the peas and the spring
onion between your bread cases
then slowly pour the egg mixture
into each one. Be careful not to
overfill the cases!

6 Sprinkle the last bit of the grated
cheese over each tart and pop in the
oven for 15 minutes or until they
are set and golden . . . Mmm!

For 6 friends

Florentine's Home-made pink Lemonade with Fresh Berry Ice Cubes

For the ice cubes
A big handful of fresh berries

For the lemonade
A big bottle of fizzy water
5 lemons
The juice from a packet of cooked beetroot (not pickled!)
6 tbsp runny honey

1 Pop one or two berries into each compartment of an ice cube tray. Fill with water and freeze overnight.

2 Pour the fizzy water into a big jug and squeeze in the juice of four lemons.

3 Carefully chop the last lemon into chunks (with the peel still on!) and add to the water.

4 Snip the corner off the packet of beetroot and carefully pour the juice into the water.

5 Stir in the honey and add your beautiful berry ice cubes just before you serve to your thirsty friends.